Hatred. Hidden.

A Psychological Short Story

Smoke & Dust Books

Hatred. Hidden. © Dan Thompson 2016
All rights reserved

First published 2016 by Smoke & Dust Books
First compiled and told within *The Caseworker's Memoirs* first published 2013

All characters, names and events featured in this publication, other than those clearly in the public domain, are entirely fictional. Any resemblance to any person, organisation, place or thing, living or dead, is purely coincidental.

No part of this book may be reproduced in any form other than that in which it was purchased and without the written permission of the author.

danthompsonauthor.com

ISBN-13: 978-1536845471

Hatred. Hidden.

Jane,

To my friend!

Thanks for your support!

Dan
2016

Also by Dan Thompson

The Black Petal

Here Lies Love

Ana's Trial

The Caseworker's Memoirs

Poetry

Life is all but a vast array of Colours

For Malcolm, I enjoyed our time together. I may revisit you, one day. For now, have a rest. You've deserved it

Homosexuality exists in 450 species ... Homophobia is found in only one.

- Unknown

If people cared more about men holding guns than men holding hands the world would be a better place.

- Unknown

Hatred. Hidden.

THE BRONZE BELL JANGLED AS the man opened the shop door and he ventured inside. It had been stiff to open; one of those old wooden doors, plaster flaking slightly, where you had to give it a shoulder shove. A sweet perfumed scent gently filled his nostrils, reminding him of his wife's love of joss sticks. He smiled. At least this was a more natural aroma and didn't cling to the back of this throat like acid reflux. Not that he could have admitted that to her. A clout round the ear would have been his reward for that smart comment, or perhaps a jab in the side.

Mark tucked his hands into his smart black trousers, crease always ironed in, and surveyed the florist's displays and shop floor. Cream lilies stood proud amongst a backdrop of delicate-looking freesia and violet chrysanthemums. Perhaps a little too understated. Not what he was after. He needed to make more of an announcement. She deserved it, he knew. Tall sunflowers caught his attention, goldenrod yellow, a particular favourite of hers. She would love them. They reminded him of their son's school painting blu-tacked to the fridge.

He wandered in, venturing past the terracotta-potted ferns and stopped at some scarlet poinsettias. The petals felt like mini velvet scarves. He envisioned a bunch, smiling from their elegant vase as the whole family tucked into a delicious Sunday meal. His stomach growled just thinking about the meal. Of course, there had to be homemade yorkshire puddings. It was Christmas after all.

'Can I help you?' A blonde assistant sprang up from behind the counter.

Mark approached her, all smile and teeth. 'Hi, erm … yes.' He glanced for her name badge. 'Shirley, store owner. That's an original name. I've got to say, I would never have guessed Shirley.' He leaned against the counter.

Shirley beamed at him for a few moments as if not knowing how to respond. She blushed. 'It was a nightmare when I was a teenager. I used to tell everyone I was Shelly. Now, it's kinda retro, you know? My mum loved *Are You Being Served?* apparently.'

'Right,' Mark chuckled. He couldn't help but eye her rotund face and unusually auburn eyes that seemed to illuminate the more she blushed. He couldn't stifle the grin in knowing that, even though he used Just For Men occasionally, he still had *it*. And he was sure it had nothing to do with the liberal amounts of eau de toilette he drowned himself in the gym's changing room half an hour earlier.

'So,' Shirley broke the silence, 'anything I can help you with?'

'I was hoping to buy my wife some flowers.'

'Sure. Are they for a special occasion?'

He shook his head. 'I just fancied buying her a little something to make her smile.'

'How nice of you! Did you have anything in mind?'

It was only now, after he had taken his focus from her looks and tempting décolletage, that Mark realised she had a thick Australian accent. 'Well actually,' he said, walking back across the well-lit shop, 'she does love sunflowers.'

'Good choice, although nothing says I love you more than a dozen red roses. Perhaps you'd like a smell?'

He leant towards the vase of roses she had slipped from one of the windowsills.

'They smell wonderful,' he lied. He couldn't smell a single note. Perhaps the congregation of flora around the room stole their subtleness, but he did run a finger over the petals. 'Are they not a tad bit too predictable though?'

'Maybe a little,' she admitted. 'But you know, no woman can resist a tall, handsome man bearing roses.'

'OK.' He succumbed to the woman's flirty charm and pulled out his wallet. 'I'll take them.'

HE SUCKED IN HIS GUT, pressed out his chest, and stood shoulder width apart. The roses were skilfully hidden behind his back and he waited patiently for the front door to be opened. Lucy's sultry voice could be heard from the living room; he had to force his face to stay serious, but that was proving difficult.

His wife's petite face eyed him through the door's glass with a hint of suspicion. 'What are you ringing the bell for, silly?' she asked as she pulled open the door slowly. She leaned against the corner of the door, propping her weight on it with her bare foot keeping the door still. He knew she was hinting at him, again, that the bloody thing needed re-varnishing.

'I have a surprise for you.'

He deliberately made her wait. The electricity between them made his stomach ache. Even after fifteen years of marriage, no flirty florist could pull him away from Lucy, not even a racy Australian accent. Lucy's eyes tightened and she pouted. The fine indent of crow's feet wasn't a sign of old age in his eyes, but more a banner of experience. *She thinks I'm playing a game.* She pressed her chin to her chest and blinked puppy dog eyes at him.

'OK. You've got me,' he surrendered.

'You always fall for that look. Eyelashes get you every time!'

Mark swung both hands round and presented the flowers to his wife. 'I love you.'

Lucy giggled, carefully taking the roses. She pressed her button nose into the gift-wrapped bouquet. 'What are these for, you soppy sod?'

She's perfect, Mark thought. Beautiful figure, gorgeous personality, and best of all, his. Her smile was infectious and he watched her intently. 'A cheeky excuse for me to see that yummy smile of yours,' he said, stepping into the doorway and locking his lips against hers. He guided her backwards through the hall. 'Ooh you get me so excited,' he groaned as he pulled away.

'Well, if you want me,' she nibbled on the end of his nose, 'you'll have to catch me.'

He admired the wiggle of her behind as she ran through the magnolia hallway and into the open plan kitchen, tiptoeing around the central work-surfaces.

'You are a tease!'

She tittered and ran around the cupboards just as he circled towards her. He wanted to reclaim his prize, but she twirled and twirled, and no matter how hard he tried, Mark always found himself on the opposite side of the marble top. *She really is a tease, the little minx.*

Both husband and wife breathed heavily in sync with one another. Mark couldn't keep his gaze off her. 'I want you,' he whispered, knowing just how cheesy it sounded and not caring one bit.

Lucy replied in action, slowly unbuttoning her pale blouse, one button after another, taking as much time as she wanted. He caught a glimpse of pink lingerie. 'Look what you are missing out on, standing all the way over there.'

Mark hardened; he wasted no time and lunged over the marble island, trapping his wife inside long muscular arms. With a tilt of her neck with his face, he growled into her ear, caressing the lobe with a quivering tongue. He followed a trail, down past her shoulders, over her chest, finally stopping on his knees and planting fast pecks across her navel.

The bouquet of roses dropped to the floor beside him in a dash of colour. Lucy thrusted his head and face against her body. The goosebumps along her arms excited him further. Mark cusped some of the petals;

starting at her bellybutton, he stroked his wife's body with the supple petals and relished in her moans, smelling her saccharine skin as he ventured upwards. The cloudy stretchmarks on her sides and the bottom of her torso brought back the memories of a sexually active pregnancy for both of them. Nine years had passed since then, but he wasn't put off by their obviousness. They represented another notch to her name: wife, lover, mother, provider. He loved them all in equal measure.

Lucy forced another slippery kiss before leading her husband upstairs into the bedroom. She took control, and piece by piece, she ripped his clothes off his body. Her animalistic urges surprised him a little, especially as she tore open his shirt, taking no care whatsoever with the buttons. But her teeth against his nipples sent tingles down his legs and he threw the shirt across the room. He catapulted back onto the kingsize bed and Lucy fumbled with his shoes and socks. No man in the history of the world, he thought, ever looked sexy trying to remove their socks and shoes. But at least removing him from his trousers brought the fun right back.

With only his boxer shorts left, Lucy kept his gaze by removing the last of her own underclothing and straddled on top of him. Her fingernails over his chest were sharp, but added tantalising contrast to her grinding in his lap, his arms thrust behind his head. A slight wetness soaked through his boxers; he surrendered to the lust completely. He whipped them off without a second thought and gasped as she sat back atop and slipped him inside.

They rocked back and forth, Lucy allowing her husband to caress her breasts. The thrill of the grind and the concentration he put into rubbing his thumbs over her hard, dark nipples was enough to bring him to climax almost instantly, but he breathed and tilted his hips into the bed to slow Lucy down.

But as they locked eyes, their connection deepened, and a tidal rush overcame him. As quickly as they had started, they both held one another close, enjoying the comfort of each other's heartbeat. The world outside could wait; this was their time, and neither Lucy nor Mark allowed any interruption to bother them. Give me five minutes, he thought, and then I'm going to ravish you properly.

'NO, NO, NO, NO!' LUCY shrieked as she clambered off the bed, grabbing Mark's shirt and darting down the stairs.

'What's up?' Mark ran after her.

'The bloody chicken.'

The acrid smell of burnt poultry seemed to confirm her doubts. The chicken was charred and black and ruined. Lucy ran her hands through her already dishevelled hair. 'Bloody hell! It's a disaster.'

Mark clutched her hand and kissed her forehead. 'Hey, don't worry. We'll just order take out. What will Humphrey want?'

'You know he hates it when you call him that.'

'He knows I'm only joking.'

'I never get it.'

'He looks like a young Humphrey Bogart. We should totally enter him into competitions. A right good lookalike.'

'He's only nine! I am not turning our son into one of those glammed up, bratty kids. And I'm definitely not becoming a pageant mum.'

'You'd totally kick their arses. You could pull out their fake eyelashes and rip off the ridiculous hair extensions. In fact all you'd need to do is show them a mirror and they'd melt! The reflection of those I've-got-a-liver-condition fake tans would be like the Medusa effect.'

Lucy smirked. 'I thought Medusa turned people into stone. I think you're confusing mythology with the Wicked Witch of the West.'

Mark shrugged.

'Anyway, Colby's staying over with a friend tonight.' She grumbled loudly into his chest and mocked a fake sob. 'The poor chicken.'

'Well that settles it. Let's get our glad rags on. I'm taking you out!'

Lucy wiped her chestnut hair from out her eyes and shook with anticipation. She ran back upstairs, taking two steps at a time, as giddy as a schoolgirl. Mark laughed to himself before shaking his head at the chicken.

'Sorry, girl. Looks like you missed out tonight.' He covered the charred thing with a damp tea towel.

THE HEADLAMPS OF THE CAR lit up the Christmas baubles hanging in the High Street; the glowing snowflakes and animated reindeers encapsulated a warm, inviting, if not bitter, winter's evening. The sun had long set, but these shorter days gave birth to lively night outings before settling down in front of a crackling fire, drinking moreish hot chocolate with a healthy side of melting marshmallows. A dash of whiskey in the chocolate never hurt anyone either.

Mark and Lucy walked arm in arm across the carpark with almost a skip in their step, and entered the Italian restaurant. The bistro was pleasantly quiet. In the corner, a man with a balding top, dexterously played the piano, skipping his fingers from key to key, not paying attention to anyone inside the place. For such a small eatery, the bistro's owners had used the space well. *One ... two ...* Mark counted the tables – eleven in total, and yet it didn't feel cramped. Some of the tables were placed at symmetrical angles, a few almost hidden in the alcoves. They were already taken. A dozen or so poinsettias added festive spirit, their scarlet splicing well against the dark oak beams and the warm glow of the candlelight. Perhaps Shirley had recommended them, Mark thought.

Garlic permeated through the air, deliciously making Mark's stomach growl in anticipation. Italian restaurants always had such a fantastic aroma to them: complicated, cultured, multi-layered, as if there was something for everyone and any age. Chinese takeaways had a greasy air to them, and Indian restaurants reminded Mark of the sweaty gym changing rooms where men walked around, swinging in all directions. Italian was the only way to go.

The windows had a nice coating of snow spray against them, much more professional than Humphrey's overkill with their tree. Whereas here the fake snow had been templated into snowflakes, their son had gone crazy with it as if it was silly string, ending up looking like cheap deodorant that flaked everywhere when the cap had been broken.

Yes, the bistro was more to Mark's liking. Mature, adult, homely. A dead cert 'no kids allowed'. The kind of place that had the racks behind the bar with one hundred and one different kinds of spirits and liquors on offer. He was ready for something to warm the back of his throat.

'What's taking your fancy?' Mark asked after glancing flippantly from food menu to wine menu. The waiter had sat them furthest away from the door, which was exactly how Mark liked it. He loved to get a sense of a place. Free to turn and see everyone and anyone.

'Apart from you, you mean?' Lucy replied.

'Cheeky!'

While Lucy perused the drinks menu, Mark surveyed the other diners. He was never sure why, but it was a game he enjoyed – taking in the appearance and then, rather stereotypically, guessing at what their occupation was. Of course, he could never find out if he guessed right, how close he was, but that didn't bother him. The thrill of closing down his surroundings to just one person and living solely inside his own head was a pleasure he assumed very few could experience. He could actually hear his own voice: sophisticated, with a charming wit. He liked it, even when he heard it on phone answer machines and iPhone videos. He wasn't ashamed.

Poor Lucy, he thought. The 'men can't multitask' stereotype didn't quite work for him. He *chose* to zone out when she babbled on, playing his mental game. He had no interest in last night's episode of *Eastenders*, or what gossip she'd overheard in the school playground, or even that there was a deal on salmon at the supermarket. Why would she think he would be interested? No, he'd rather concentrate on other matters. He'd nearly perfected the zoning out with the nods and mmm-hmmms in all the right places. He needed some liberties at least.

He tidied up after himself, actually put the dirty clothes *inside* the wash basket instead of on top of it, he put the toilet seat down after use. He was even dignified and didn't watch TV laid on the settee with a stray hand shoved down his boxers for a comforting fiddle.

No, Lucy can't complain. Without so much as moving his head, using his eyes only, he glanced over to the first alcove. Just a woman by herself. Short, dark blonde hair and copper highlights. She was staring into her wine. Not wine, Mark reassessed, it was the colour of urine. Lambrini, most likely.

Hairdresser. She had to be.

In another alcove two men chatted with pints. One had a lager, the other a bitter. More froth. Both men cleanly shaven. The one of the left had obvious streaks of grey, while the other one was more salt and pepper. Top buttons undone, but ties still high. They had possibly only just arrived too.

Bankers. Or accountants. Estate agents at a push. Hmmm. Not estate agents, he thought. They tended to be younger nowadays, working for a basic salary, relying on bonuses and quotas being reached. And this wasn't London or Birmingham. Bankers a tad too unrealistic and upper class. *Accountants*.

'Mark. Mark!'

'Hmm, what?' Lucy stared at him with narrowed eyes.

'What's up? You're a million miles away.'

'Sorry. What did you say?'

'I said … I think I'll try one of the cocktails. There's a couple taking my fancy.'

'Get them all.' Mark shifted in his seat, losing track of where he was.

'All? I don't think so. How will that look? What you having?'

'Erm …' Mark fumbled for the menu still closed on the table. 'Probably just an IPA or something. You know me.' He wasn't one of those pretentious people who drank elderflower cider with mint, or lemon zest lager, or tequila and baobab fruit and squirrel shit mixed in and all that crap. How could people drink that rubbish? Ale or hard spirits, that was him.

He pretended to read the menu, but took no notice of the words. When Lucy had gone back to the menu, and then picking up the food one accompanying it, Mark returned to his game. *Lambrini hairdresser, done her*. He leant to see past the waiter scurrying about and sighed. A couple was exiting the bistro before he had had a chance to fit them in somewhere. He sucked in air and exhaled loudly, but thankfully, Lucy didn't seem to notice.

On a table just to their right, Mark noticed two men. How he'd missed them before he couldn't tell, but they would do perfectly. They joked and laughed in an unobtrusive way, not really drawing any attention to themselves. Possibly celebrating an early Christmas. Leftovers of tortellini sat on both plates, but the bottle of rosé was practically empty. They were going to be a bit tougher, or at least the toughest of the night so far.

The waiter trundled past and Mark suddenly caught sight of the men playing with one another's feet under the table. The blonde haired, and leaner of the two, snorted in some sort of flirty embarrassment. Mark's neck prickled, his arms itchy too. He scratched at them and his hairline. A hot wave surged from his gut, up into his chest. He could taste the acid in his stomach rise into his throat. It gurgled, he coughed, as if trying to quash the coming tidal wave of emotion.

Were they looking into each other's eyes? In that *sort of way?*

He couldn't take his eyes off them now. He needed more proof. And as if they had heard him, the other – mousy haired, a touch of ginger in his beard and moustache – stroked the hand of his date.

Caught in their trap, Mark's breath stuck hard in his throat and his face burned with a distressing flush.

'So, you decided?' Lucy asked and reached over to stroke her husband's hand. She really did look happy to be out and about, Mark noticed.

Still, he couldn't shake the awful dread. He pulled his hand away abruptly, leaving Lucy's to thud onto the table. He faffed with his collar, struggling to loosen the buttons.

'Sorry. Sorry, it's just too damn hot in here!'

He shot his arm out, flapping for the water jug unsteadily. He gulped it down, thankful for its coolness as it washed down the bile. As he held his head back, still gulping in large mouthfuls, the two men joked again. They erupted into a playful laughter. Mark strained to see through the clear glass; one – it could have been the mousy haired one – wiped away tears of hilarity. Mark noticed his almost oriental eyes. He didn't look foreign though. He needed to focus on his breathing.

'I think I'll have the prawn risotto,' Lucy added to his thoughts, obviously ignoring his earlier outburst. 'But … the seabass sounds delicious too. It's got samphire with it. Do you think I could swap the new potatoes for mash?'

'Order what you bloody well want. You always do! What does my opinion count for?' Mark barked back.

Lucy twitched at his outburst. Lights buzzed in front of him as the anger fizzled his hearing like TV static. Muffles from the adjacent tables amalgamated into elongated drones. He shuddered and felt sick.

'Mark,' Lucy croaked. 'Don't speak to me like that.' Her neck reddened, turning orange in the candlelight.

Mark dabbed at his watering eyes with a napkin. 'I'm sorry, love. Honestly. I don't know what's come over me. I just feel … a little off.'

Lucy wasn't having any of it, it seemed, and shook her head with disbelief. 'I know you better than that. Something's bothering you.'

'I,' he went to reply, but noticed the two lovers leave instead. They scooted money onto a tin tray. *They look just like ordinary people*. He watched, disgusted, as both men headed for a side door. Mark knew it wasn't the exit. His heart pounded. *Boom … boom … boom*. A black stick figure spoke loudly, bolted to the wooden door. He couldn't believe it.

'I can't believe it,' he said aloud.

'What?'

'In a public place. So typical to do it in a toilet. So disgusting.' He rubbed the bridge of his nose and frowned around the bistro. Things were getting out of hand. He was losing himself to the anger, to the revulsion and abhorrence, to the fear. He usually dealt with it accordingly. Here, in such a public place, and in front of Lucy too, well, that was not on.

Two boys, roughly Colby's age, swung their legs off stools, playing on handheld gaming systems. The *thud thud* of the stools struck a nerve, a vein in his temple throbbed.

'The children. What if they walk in?'

'What children? Mark, you're not making sense. Talk to me.'

He brushed her hand aside again, rubbing at his legs, knees, neck, feeling the sweat trickle from his armpit and down his side. It felt wet and humid to touch. Damn, why did he wear a light coloured shirt? People would think he was a vagrant, or an alcoholic, or something even more degrading. He needed to show them he was none of those things, show Lucy he had her back, show the innocent children he could protect them from such vile activity.

He went to stand, attempting to confront the two of them in the gents, but faltered mid step and flopped back onto the chair. He didn't want to see any of that. The gents wasn't exactly the best sights in the world: piss stained urinals or rusty troughs, half dissolved urinal cakes that smelt like cheap mints and lemon disinfectant. A condom machine probably half broken into. Most sold those fad sexual enhancement pills nowadays anyway. A blue bill for stamina and performance. He scoffed; as if he needed them. Besides, what did he care, you could get a johnny online now, a box full of them.

He lunged for Lucy's clean napkin and spat into it. Their sordid behaviour had turned his thoughts to urinals and condoms. They were infectious. He spat again.

What's taking them so long? They must be at it like backward animals! They should be out by now, it shouldn't take that long.

He scrutinised his watch, gritted his teeth, and felt the bones in his jaw grind.

And finally, the two men exited the toilets calmly. Mousy, as Mark now referred to him, rubbed his hands down his beige chinos. The blonde slipped his hands into his pockets. They shimmied past the tables, heading for the exit, like ghosts. No one looked up from their tables at them, paid them any attention. And just like that, they were gone, like mist evaporating in the cool, winter air.

The buzz had took hold now though, like a hand clutching his throat. He was suffocating under the pressure of sitting there, doing nothing, or playing the hero and taking action. Mark tapped his foot. Lucy babbled something, her hands waving at the far reaches of his vision's periphery. If only he could swat the annoying fly back into her seat and enjoy the meal he would be paying for, the ungrateful bitch. Money, that's all he was to her. She was no more than a whore who bled him dry.

His fingernails were sharp against his cheek as he raked them down. What was becoming of him? He never thought of Lucy like that. A demon had possessed his mind, it needed purging. As soon as the children laughed in silly fits over their game, Mark shot out his seat, knocking the jug of water over at the same time. He vaguely heard it clutter onto the floor, Lucy's voice too, but he didn't have time for her nagging questions. He darted for the entrance. They had to be stopped.

The nippy air slammed into him like an inebriated spirit, but he staggered left and right, searching. A car down opened. A burgundy taxi had an illuminated light on top, flashing intermittently as if it was on the verge of breaking. There they were, he saw. Beside the taxi, like shadows in a dark alley. They joined, faces together, kissing. Their warm breath wispy, rising into the night sky. Before clambering into the taxi, one wrapped a dark scarf around the other. They kissed again, waved, and parted. As he walked away down the high street, Mark realised it was Mousy who hadn't got into the taxi.

Mark marched after him, hearing the taxi's mechanical thrum rotating through his head. 'Oi! You!' he bellowed, reaching Mousy and swinging him around. He held him by the scruff of his coat and scarf, ripping at it violently.

'Whoa, mate. What's the problem?' His voice was nervy.

'You are my problem.' Mark spat in his face, again and again, over and over, making sure it covered his eyes.

Mousy struggled to get free, wiping frantically at his eyes and pulling away. Mark was having none of it. He threw a punch into Mousy's stomach, satisfied with the resulting grunt, and pushed him to the already icy ground. He kicked the downed man, wherever they connected. Back, stomach, head, he didn't care. As long as the blows were fast, one after the other.

'You disgust me,' he grunted, 'all you lot, your entire kind.'

'Please,' Mousy quavered, but his pleading was lost in between the groans and obscenities.

'How does Little Miss Princess like that, eh? Little Miss Puff. Feel good does it. Yeah you like that, don't you? One man touching another, taking it night after night'

A screech of tyres echoed somewhere behind them.

If a whisper had tried to bring about guilt, it failed. Blood thirsty adrenaline filled his veins and spurred him on. There was a crack of ribs and coughs of blood, like the spark and sizzle of fireworks. He had forgotten how riveting this felt, like a Templar revolting against the political correctness of a slave society. The man at the gym who had looked at him funny in the shower. The sound of his head cracking against the tiles could never be forgotten. He had stored it away for moments of pleasure, along with the couple he had come across as he jogged through the park, alongside the river. They never knew what was coming when he rammed one into the river itself before landing a few good blows to the other. He had broken his Bluetooth headphones that day, Lucy had bought him some new ones for Father's Day as a replacement. And he had gotten away with them all too, like divine justice allowing him the cloak of invisibility to carry out a purge.

'Gay marriage,' he laughed. 'What a joke. This country has gone mad. What gives you the right to have these things? A good stoning, that's what's needed. All of you, put against the wall and stoned. Like the Muslims do it.'

Mark was thrown backwards, and he stumbled to keep upright. The ice on the ground was like cold fire to the tips of his fingers, but he managed to grab hold of a lamppost. The blonde lover had returned, screaming something at him. Mark chided himself for not paying more attention; he had bloody gone in the taxi, he assumed.

'Steve? Steve?' The man knelt down and wiped blood from Mousy's face. 'Please, Steve.'

Mark hovered closer and saw the mess, the blood, the broken teeth. Mousy was unrecognisable. He lay there, silently, unmoving.

'What have you done?' the man cried up at him. 'What have you done? Happy now? Feel big, and hard, proud man?'

'You fucking little shit,' Mark spat back, leaning in to punch out.

'Mark!'

He bolted around. A crowd stared at him, some with hands over their mouths, a husband shielding his wife. The children stared, gobsmacked, ignoring the ushers from one of the waiters desperately trying to get them inside, away from him, like he was a disease. Lucy was there too, frozen to the spot like some mannequin. He jogged over.

'It's OK. I've stopped them. You don't have to worry about anything. I've sorted it all.'

But Lucy was crying. Mascara blackened her eyes and streaked her cheeks. She rubbed her stomach nervously. 'Mark … what have you done?'

'Me,' he scoffed, 'me. They. Them. It was sickening.' He pointed over to them, Mousy still quiet on the ground, the other sobbing like a little girl, Mark thought. 'Look at them. It's not normal. It's not right.' He edged towards her, wanting to put an arm around her, to stroke her hair and kiss her cheek. Wipe away the mascara stains before they turned her entire face black.

'No,' she gasped. She slipped off a high heel and lunged it at him. He ducked, but it still whacked his shoulder. 'Don't come near me. Have you killed him? God, you've killed him, haven't you. Killed an innocent man.'

'Innocent! Have you gone mad, woman.' He couldn't comprehend his wife's attitude. 'Why aren't you here, by my side? I've just saved those children, those two *innocent* children.'

The diners shook their heads at him and Lucy cried. One of the barmen approached him and tried to tackle him to the ground, but Mark scooted onto the road away from them.

'Why are you looking at me like that? What is wrong with all of you?'

Sirens cut through the frightened crowd. Mark's stomach suddenly ached with a feeling he couldn't recognise, like an end was swiftly approaching. His mind clouded and confused the reality. *What was happening?* Stars stared down at him like eyes, like judge and jury. He held out his shaking hands, but they were clean. No blood. He wasn't tainted by death, or sin, like the shadows in the distance. He was a saviour, a goodwill ambassador and hero.

Fury was now satisfied.

PSYCHIATRIC REPORT OF PATIENT

HM PRISON FERRYTHORPE

MARK SANDERSON, 41 YEARS, MALE, PRISONER NO #45587

Report by Malcolm White

Fear, terror, and an instantaneous urge to remove oneself from an object or situation will usually define a phobia. Homophobia doesn't fall under the normal restraints that define phobias, and homophobia isn't necessarily a fear per se, but the uncomfortable emotion same sex activity causes certain people is very much the same thing.

The actual phobia itself is not just a mental anguish, but also one that is flamed, and in some instances, created by the cultural and sociological world. Background, upbringing, geographical location, all play a part in nurturing the obsession, and it is just as current today as it was ten years ago. I imagine it to be like an awful fashion trend that comes around every decade. Society seems to go through a period of peace with it, but then something will happen and the fear comes right back. It is my opinion that

Mark's actions will undoubtedly lead to similar cases happening around the country.

Mark was perfect, so out of character and *it's just not like him at all*: all testimonials from friends and family. I'm afraid this is natural and fits in with homophobia cases well. Mark could easily have hidden his hate, especially if friends and family were entirely heterosexual. His acting out came in secret, until it consumed him so much he acted out in the case which led to his arrest.

Homophobia isn't an illness, contrary to some other leading psychiatric reports, and therefore cannot be cured. So curing his *problem* wasn't the issue here, but instead, the education of individuality was paramount for Mark's rehabilitation. Stereotypical, generalised stigmas needed challenging in Mark's case.

By using video footage and images, I was able to witness the levels of anger and awkwardness someone's sexuality caused within Mark. Mark preferred to close his eyes, ignore my questioning, and not pay any attention to me whatsoever. I tried to educate him on genetic reasoning: that sexuality wasn't a chosen lifestyle. By killing a young man, Mark had eradicated an evil from the world, he had said.

Material provided from the archives proved ineffectual too. An interview played to Mark where a man described the mental torture of being homosexual only caused revulsion in Mark. The interviewee went on to admit that if given a choice, he would certainly have chosen to be heterosexual.

Religion didn't seem to play a role in his phobia. I've delved deep into Mark's life, probing for information and he seems to find religion a joke, in my opinion.

It isn't for me to judge Mark on his crimes, or enforce my personal opinion on him, but merely ask questions to better understand his motives. A serious crime has been committed, but prison life is not helping my understanding of Mark. He's shutting down, withdrawing within himself. He's admitted prison life is like living in medieval times with wardens intimidating inmates with bars and doors. I suspect something is happening to him within his cell, but he will not share it with me. I've given him ample opportunity. It is my educated guess that he himself is being sexually abused in some way; a cruel twist of fate it seems.

I also wasn't surprised to note that the phobia only manifested itself with male homosexuality. Sexual acts between women didn't result in the same hatred. Lesbianism was a viewing pleasure for Mark. It is often the case in male patients. Hypocritical brain processes lead me to believe that it certainly is a cultural reasoning behind the homophobia. It is so rooted in him I do not feel I've made much progress with rehabilitation and it is my medical opinion that he will never change his mind. Placing him among open homosexuals will only result in potential harm to the gay people involved.

If released from prison after his sentence, I feel he will act out again, possibly even in secret to satiate his need to 'do the right thing'. His 1950's view of the world makes him a danger to many who oppose him. I feel Mark is a prime example of his generation. Education is needed in schools, informing pupils of differences early on, halting any niggling phobias before they become a much bigger problem down the line. Perhaps one day, just how racism has started to be overturned in this country, then so will this issue.

Mark was not the perfect man who lost it all as the media have reported the case. He is clever and sophisticated, and could very much resemble the man next door, a neighbour two floors up, or the man in the queue at the bank. Homophobia is very much hidden unless acted out in public among witnesses.

Author's Note

To some, Mark's acting out and his violent conduct may seem like I support or encourage such behaviour against not just the LGBT community, but other human beings in general. That is not true. I abhor violence. As an earlier quote I cannot find the author of says: 'If people cared more about men holding guns than men holding hands the world would be a better place' – well, that is a statement I do fully support.

Even though Mark doesn't wield a gun, I wouldn't put it past him to use one if one popped up on the street next to him.

Homophobia is rife the world over and instead of telling a story from a victim's point of view, where readers would feel sorry for such a person, I wanted to recount a story from the attacker's mind set, to attempt to scare, make readers feel uncomfortable, to get them to question their own beliefs.

I hope you enjoyed my short story. A short, unbiased review on the website you bought it from would mean the world to me. I would hug you for doing so, but you might then catch my cold, which wouldn't be fair. I would also love you to sign up to my newsletter too, which you can do on my website.

You can join me on:

FACEBOOK: facebook.com/theblackpetal
TWITTER: @dan_pentagram
WEBSITE: danthompsonauthor.com

HERE LIES LOVE
Available in eBook, Paperback & Audio

Would death be less painful than life?

When she is sold by her father, Abbey discovers that nightmares can occur when you're awake. Trapped inside a wooden cage, Abbey is forced to listen to the horrors and atrocities above; time ticking down until it is her turn. But Abbey isn't prepared to become a victim; she will escape.

Although, what Abbey isn't prepared for, is how harsh and unfair the world can be. With the sun turning its back on humanity long ago, life gives no opportunity. The only thing Abbey can do is learn to survive. To exist. And that means stealing any opportunity that comes her way. Haunted by the unpleasant memories bestowed upon her only nurtures Abbey's paranoia, until she realises that to truly live in the world, she must confront the person who was responsible for her misfortune – her father.

Here Lies Love is a NA Dystopian tale of actuality, of facing up to the fact that love comes in many guises. Can Abbey find the one glimmer of hope or will she be overcome with the darkness of revenge?

☆☆☆☆☆ - "*a truly harrowing tale made worthwhile by a beautifully compelling protagonist*" - Jack Croxall, Bestselling Amazon author of the *Tethers* trilogy.

THE BLACK PETAL
AVAILABLE IN EBOOK & PAPERBACK

Acclaimed author of *Here Lies Love*, Dan Thompson, returns with an epic fantasy being described as *A Game of Thrones* for Teens!

Come and Enter this magical tale of fantasy and myth, battles and warriors, and meet the host of memorable characters.

Jack, a teenager from our present, and Blake, a Victorian assassin, are plucked from their homes and awaken in a new land; a realm of fantasy and myth. Drawn into a war between two rival races, they must each choose allies. Jack wants to get home. Blake wants revenge.

An Oracle has persuaded the Amazon Queen that a black petal will summon a powerful god who can grant them victory. A prophecy told long ago tells of a boy from another time who can discover this petal and the Amazon Queen is certain Jack is this boy. She offers him freedom and a way home in exchange.

Will Jack reach the petal in time or will he succumb to the yapping jaws of the mysterious creatures chasing him? And what of Blake? What is the connection between Jack and the assassin that will surely shape their future?

The Black Petal is the first adventure in an exciting new trilogy.

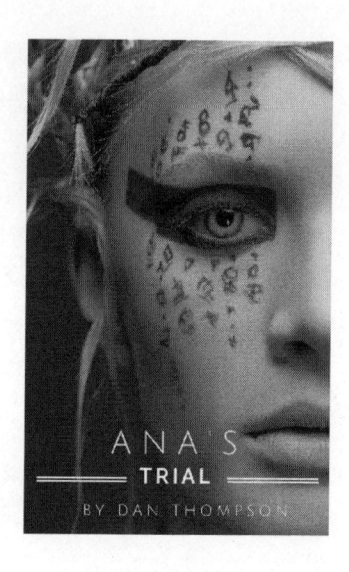

ANA'S TRIAL
AVAILABLE IN EBOOK

In a time before the pyramids and the Pharaohs and the glory, Egypt was home to nomadic travellers. Ana is one such person, and heir to a tribe she doesn't want to lead. She's but fifteen years and longs for exploration. But duty is knocking on her door.

A trial awaits her. The weight of her father's expectations is heavy.

Witness the magic of a prepharaonic Egypt, and see if Ana will succeed in this short story from the acclaimed young adult author of *The Black Petal*, Dan Thompson.

Printed in Great Britain
by Amazon